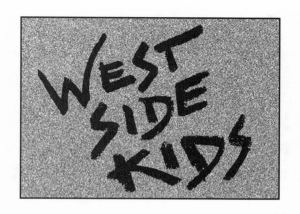

WEST SIDE KIDS

THE BIG IDEA

ELLEN SCHECTER
Illustrated by **BOB DORSEY**

Bank Street

Hyperion Paperbacks for Children
New York

For my mother,
who helped me dream of gardens.
And my daughter,
who helped this one grow

—E. S.

First Hyperion Paperback edition 1996

Text ©1996 by Bank Street College of Education.
Illustrations ©1996 by Bob Dorsey.

Printed in the United States of America.

1 3 5 7 9 10 8 6 4 2

The artwork for this book is prepared using pencil.
The text for this book is set in 12-point Berling.

Library of Congress Cataloging-in-Publication Data

Schecter, Ellen.
      The big idea / written by Ellen Schecter.
         p.   cm.—(The West Side kids ; 1)
      Summary: Eight-year-old Luz Mendes is determined to turn a run-down vacant lot into a garden like the one her grandfather had in Puerto Rico, but she must convince her neighbors to help.
      ISBN 0-7868-2085-3 (lib. bdg.) — ISBN 0-7868-1043-2 (pbk.)
      [1. Community gardens—Fiction.   2. Gardens—Fiction.   3. City and town life—New York (N.Y.)—Fiction.]   4. Puerto Ricans—Fiction.   5. New York (N.Y.)—Fiction.]   I. Title.   II. Series.
      PZ7.S3423P1   1996
      [Fic]—dc20   95-4823

Other books in the West Side Kids series

Don't Call Me Slob-o

THE WEST SIDE KIDS' NEIGHBORHOOD

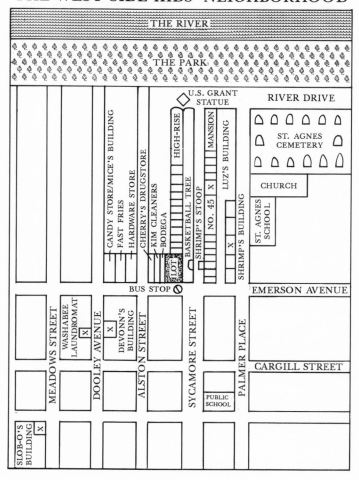

CONTENTS

WHAT IF?

I WISH I could fly—right off this hard cement sidewalk to a place full of green trees and bright flowers. Especially now that it's spring.

Instead, I skate over to my friend Rosie's window and whistle twice. She lives on the second floor of my building. It's our own special signal: one low, one high.

Rosie's there in a second, like she's been waiting for me. She opens her window and waves. Everything about Rosie is small and blond except her blue eyes and her glasses. Everything about me is tall and curly and light brown.

"Hi, Luz!" Rosie calls. Her big glasses flash in the sun.

"I'm going to the bodega to buy rice and onions before Mami gets home from work," I call up to her. "Want to do something tomorrow?"

"Okay!" Rosie grins. "I'll see you then."

I skim down Sycamore Street, doing fancy steps on the wide, smooth sidewalk. I can feel the wind in my face, and the *bump-bump* of my blades on the cement.

I pretend I'm an Olympic racer and go whirling

past houses in ice-cream colors: vanilla, strawberry, and mint. I live in the chocolate one with the peeling paint.

Lots of people are out on our street today in the warm sun and soft air.

"Hey, Mike, DeVonn," I call. "Hi!"

"What's up, Luz?" DeVonn yells back.

Mike Donnelly and DeVonn Chapman are two guys my age. They're warming up for opening day. Of the West Side Little League, that is. You'd think they play for the Yankees, they act like they're such big deals.

"Hey, Mike, let me past!" I shout. Mike thinks he owns the whole sidewalk. I have to yell again before he moves one single inch.

DeVonn pretends like he's going to tackle me, then steps out of the way with that big grin of his. I skate a fast circle around them and zoom off down the street. I pass some dead-looking trees in tiny plots of dirt that look harder than cement. For about the thousandth time, I wish we had more trees and flowers on our block.

¡Mira! Look at Shrimp Pazzalini sitting on his favorite stoop, watching Mike and DeVonn, hoping for a turn to pitch. His real name is Filomeno, but we all call him Shrimp. He's probably the shortest guy on the West Side. That's why the guys never let him play. And he hates always sitting on the sidelines.

"*¡Hola, Luzita!*" That's Pony, sweeping the sidewalk. He's our favorite doorman from Number 45, the fancy building next door. His real name's Felipe, but we call him Pony 'cause of the ponytail he wears.

"*¡Buenos días!*" Pony calls out to me in Spanish, the way he does every day. And I answer in English *and* Spanish, the way I always do:

"Hi, Pony! *¡Buenos días!*"

Pony keeps sweeping in front of "his" building while he coaches Mike and DeVonn.

"Hey, Mike, put your arm into it, man. Show me some action!"

If I don't hurry, I'll never get home before Mami. But I don't feel like rushing today. Not today, when the whole world feels full of soft spring sunshine.

I slow down a little and glide past a big dude with a boom box. It's pouring rap music all up and down the street. It makes me feel like dancing! A red car zooms by blasting salsa music. It's so loud they can probably hear it way over on the East Side.

Lots of people have their windows open today to let the sunshine in and the noise out. I can hear Mrs. Hodges giving an opera-singing lesson. There's Salvie, practicing his sax. And that *bang-bang-a-bang* is my papi, fixing something up on our roof.

I cross Sycamore Street, then turn the corner past an empty lot as I jump over the cracks in the sidewalk. It only takes a minute to dash into the bodega.

I say a quick hi to Ali and Nahim, the Lebanese guys who run the store. Then I buy Mami's stuff and skate back out on the street.

Most of the time, I rush past the ugly old lot that takes up the whole corner of our block. I pretend I don't even see it. This time I stop. I take off my helmet and let the wind cool my face. And I take a really good look.

What a mess! It's about as big as a baseball diamond, and full of broken glass, old bottles, and scrunched-up cans. I can see old tires, even rusty bedsprings. And tons of trash. Even the KEEP OUT sign above the locked gate is old and rusty.

I stand there looking through the fence and . . .

. . . *I can see and smell my* abuelito's *garden back in Puerto Rico where I was born. I played there all the time when I was little. Before we moved here. Now, it's like my Lito's garden is blooming again inside my head.*

We used to play hide-and-seek together on the soft grass. The flowers were bright yellow and red and purple in the hot sun. They were way, way taller than my head. And there were bees buzzing and birds chattering high up in the cool green trees. Little tree frogs hid in the leaves and sang, "¡Coquí! ¡Coquí!"

Beep-beep! The crosstown bus blows its horn . . . and here I am on the West Side, age eight and eleven-twelfths, not just a little tiny kid in Puerto Rico.

Only now when I look in that ugly old lot, I can almost see flowers growing instead of weeds. I can

imagine nice benches all along the sides. A big vegetable garden in the middle. Maybe a sandbox for little kids.

It's almost like on TV, when they show you two pictures at once—one real, and one a dream. Sure I see the ugly old lot . . . but I can see a kind of dream garden, too.

I stare at the dead brown weeds, the junk, the graffiti names written all over the walls. And I start thinking . . .

What if we fix this place up? What if we turn it into a green place with trees and flowers? A place kids could hang out. And babies and their mamis and papis, teenagers, old people.

I squint my eyes and look even harder. I see some spiky green points poking up out of the dirt. Is that something growing?

I squint my eyes even tighter to see better. And I see a dark brown shadow slipping along by the wall.

¡Asco!—disgusting! A rat!

Just then, the number five bus groans to a stop at the corner. Uh-oh—I'm late! Maybe I can still beat Mami home.

I plop on my helmet. I do a fast, fancy turn around the corner and glide off down Sycamore Street.

MY BIG IDEA

I HURRY HOME and clomp upstairs to our fourth-floor apartment, still wearing my skates. I can't wait to tell everyone about my big idea.

On the first floor, I can smell Mrs. McCormack's corned beef and cabbage. Mm! On the second floor, I sniff the heavy smell of pea soup simmering in Rosie's kitchen. (It's not *my* favorite, but Rosie loves it!) By the time I reach the third floor, I can tell Mami is already home, frying *plátanos* as a special treat. My mouth starts to water.

Uh-oh! I say to myself. She beat me home. I ring our bell.

"Hello, Papi!"

"*¡Hola, Luzita!*" Papi lets me in and gives me a hug. Mami is already rushing around the kitchen, wearing an apron over her nurse's uniform. She takes the rice and onions, then gives me a tired smile. Papi goes back to the sink, where he's trying to fix the leaky faucet.

I wash my hands and start setting the table, which my big-shot big brother Lorenzo is using as a drum.

"I have a great idea," I say.

Lorenzo rolls his eyes the way he does whenever I

have one of my big ideas. I guess it's because of all
the times my big ideas got us in trouble. Like the
time he helped me sell three dozen boxes of Christmas candy for our church. Then I lost our list of who
bought what. Or the time I convinced him to surprise
Papi by painting our front door bright purple.

But now I just ignore Lorenzo. With a quick look
at Papi, I start telling everybody about the old lot.
About how ugly it is. About how we could turn it
into a garden—

"A garden like Lito's. Remember, Mami? How we
played there when Lorenzo and I were just little
kids?"

Lorenzo makes a face and keeps drumming his
salsa beat on the table. Mami chops onions and
throws them in the pan. They sizzle as she stirs.
There's no smell in the world as delicious as my
mami's rice and beans!

I can't tell if Lorenzo hears one word I say. He's
drumming with his eyes closed, pretending he's in a
famous Latino band. Papi glances up at me from the
sink. Mami presses her lips together, all skinny and
hard. I can tell what she's thinking.

"That old lot is dirty and dangerous, Luzita," she
says. "I don't want you going in there. Understand?"

"But, Mami—"

"Did you hear me, Luz?"

Yes, I hear. But I'm not about to give up. I turn to
Lorenzo. He's still acting like a famous drummer at

some big recording session.

"Lorenzo, stop! Tell Mami we can do it. Come on, be on my side."

"Forget it, Luz. It would take a magician to turn that pile of garbage into a garden like Lito's. So don't start talking about *we*."

"Papi?" He's my best hope. The old faucet is fixed for now. He stands at the sink, thinking, washing his hands till the soapsuds turn brown.

"Do *you* think we can turn that old lot into a garden, Papi?" I ask. "Can't you just see it full of flowers and vegetables? Maybe with a tree for resting in the shade?"

Papi answers slowly and carefully, the way he always does.

"Maybe. But you heard what your mami said, Luzita. You'd have to be very, very careful not to get hurt in there."

"Oh, I will, Papi." I give Mami a smile, then bring a big bowl of salad to the table. "Mami, I promise. I'll be very careful."

Papi dries his hands, then sits at the table. "It will be a lot of very hard work, Luz."

"Yes, I know. But I know we can do it. Come on, Papi, please say you'll help."

"*Sí*, Luzita. As long as you keep your promise to Mami."

"Lorenzito?" I give him one more try.

"Count me out, Luz. I've got important things to

do. Things about my music career!" He sees the look on my face and says a little softer, "Sorry."

"Come to the table, everyone," Mami calls. "Luz, take off your skates."

I fight with the knots in my laces. They just get tighter.

Papi comes to help. He kneels beside my chair and works at the snarls. I can smell the clean, soapy smell of his hands.

"Don't you think it would be wonderful to have a garden like Lito's?" I whisper to him.

"It's not such a bad idea, Luzita," he says. "But you need lots and lots of help. You're only eight years old."

"But Papi, I'm old enough to—"

Papi puts his rough finger gently on my lips. "If you have your heart set on it—" Papi shrugs "— it's up to you to find a way. Now sit. Eat."

If it's up to me, I tell myself, I will find a way. Somehow.

3 THE DREAM GARDEN

THE NEXT MORNING is Saturday. I start to wake up. Then I hear it raining cats and dogs. I scrunch back down under my quilt and bury my face in the warm, feathery darkness. I want to get back inside my dream again:

I'm skating in slow motion through a strange, beautiful garden. The sun is hot and yellow. Birds are singing. Giant flowers and green leaves grow way, way higher than my head.

Then Mami and I are kneeling in the soft green grass. We're planting tiny trees. They grow tall as telephone poles right before my eyes. Papi is hammering and hammering, building benches with Lito and Lorenzo. Everybody's laughing and talking, half in Spanish, half in English.

Then the sound of Papi's hammering changes into—

It's Lorenzo, drumming on the door of his room. He makes so much noise that my dream breaks into a thousand pieces.

I jerk awake in my bed. I'm not in Puerto Rico. I'm on the West Side, and it's a gloomy, rainy day. No flowers, no benches, no Lito. And, especially, no garden.

Then I think about that old lot on the corner. I can't wait to tell Rosie my idea. I jump into my clothes, gulp some juice, grab two raisin bagels, and run downstairs.

Dingdong, I ring the bell at 2F.

Rosie opens her apartment door and yawns. Her hair is fuzzy from sleeping. She's still in her old flowered pj's, but she's already wearing her glasses.

I hand her a bagel and start jabbering.

"I have a great idea, Rosie," I tell her.

"Uh-oh," Rosie says.

She thinks my big ideas mean big trouble, too. Maybe because of that time I got her to play dressup, and we spilled red nail polish all over her mom's best cocktail dress. But this idea is different.

We go in her bedroom and I tell her the whole thing.

"Can't you just see it, Rosie? We can have lettuce, tomatoes, even corn on the cob. And sunflowers! And we can make little paths outlined with stones or seashells, and put benches under all the trees. We could paint them green."

She doesn't answer, so I just keep talking.

"We'll plant pink roses—your favorite, right? And a few red ones 'cause Mami loves them. And—"

Rosie is very quiet. She takes tiny bites of her bagel and chews each bite a hundred times. But I can see her little mouth curling down at the corners. I can

tell she thinks it's a bad idea. A really bad idea.

I sigh. "Okay, Rosie. Tell me what's wrong."

She chews a little more, then swallows.

"Nobody can turn that junky lot into a garden, Luz—especially not kids. It's a mess."

I start to explain. "Well, that doesn't mean—"

But Rosie keeps talking.

"Besides, I'm moving away in July, remember?" She says it like she thinks I forgot.

How could I forget? Rosie and I have been friends ever since kindergarten. I remember the first day she moved into 2F. I bumped into her in the hallway and nearly knocked her down. When she told me last month that she had to move to Ohio because of her dad's new job, I couldn't believe it. Now I know I have to believe it. But I still don't like it any more than Rosie does.

That's why she looks so sad.

I stop thinking about the garden and start to feel sad, too, right down in the middle of my stomach. We're sitting on the edge of Rosie's bed, right near her window. The rain is over, but the sky is still all gray and gloomy. I feel as sad and gray as the sky.

"Why should I work on a garden I won't even get to enjoy?" Rosie asks. She picks a raisin out of her bagel. "Besides, I don't want us to spend all our time cleaning up some crummy old lot. Let's just have fun together, Luz. Let's go skating and play on your roof and go to the sprinklers in the playground like we always do."

"I hate that you're moving, Rosie," I say. "I don't want you to go. But you're not moving for five whole months. Meantime, we can still do all our special stuff *and* make a garden, too. It'll be fun if we do it together, Rosie. Come on!"

But I can tell Rosie still hates the whole idea. For a kid who's so small, she can be as stubborn as a grown-up. Maybe even more.

I open my mouth to say a whole list of really terrific reasons. And just then, the sun suddenly starts shining like mad all up and down Sycamore Street. We both stare out the window, watching how all the cars and stoops and old iron fences look shiny and new in the bright yellow light.

And I get another idea.

"Come on, Rosie," I say. "Get dressed. Let's go outside."

I know exactly where I want to end up.

4 TRAPPED!

ROSIE AND I run down the stairs, skipping every other step the way we like to. We run into Lorenzo, who's heading out to meet DeVonn and the guys.

Outside on our stoop, we all stop to take a look around. The air smells wet and fresh. All up and down our block, everything looks clean, even the sidewalk.

Down the block, we catch up with DeVonn, Mike, and Shrimp.

"Hi, guys," Lorenzo says. "Where you headed?"

"No place yet," DeVonn says. He runs up five steps to the top of a stoop, spreads out his arms, and jumps back down to the sidewalk. He lands on his feet, light as a cat.

"Just hanging around till Little League practice," Mike says. He jumps up and hits a NO PARKING HERE TO CORNER sign with the palm of his hand. It rings like a steel drum in a band. Shrimp jumps, too; but he misses by a mile.

"C'mon, you guys, follow me," I tell them. "I want to show you something really neat."

Lorenzo gives me a funny look but doesn't say anything.

Mike does. "Uh-oh, better watch out. We may be in big trouble. I think Luz may have another big idea."

I just ignore him.

DeVonn jumps out in front.

"Follow the leader," DeVonn calls out. "I'm leader!"

We all follow him single file and copy whatever he does. We jump two big puddles, have a pretend catch, and balance on the very edge of the curb. The water in the gutter has oil rainbows on it that flash and change in the sun.

Finally, we get to the big empty lot on the corner. And I get all tongue-tied trying to explain about the garden.

"Well, what do you think?" I ask them.

They take a look. Then they just stare at me like I'm nuts or something.

"You've got to be kidding, Luz," Mike says. "This isn't a garden. It's a disaster area."

Shrimp adds his two cents. "It's one big giant Dumpster."

"There's no way we could ever fix up this junk heap," Lorenzo says. He starts counting reasons on his fingers.

"We don't have any money. Or tools. Or enough people. And what about seeds and shovels and stuff like that? Anyway, we're just kids."

- -

"Yeah, Luz. Sorry. Count me out," DeVonn says, pretending to catch a pop-up. "Listen, I gotta go home and get my stuff for Little League. You ready, Mike?"

"Yeah," Mike says. "We're definitely outta here. Tough luck, Luz."

All the guys turn and head off down the street.

"Come on, Luz," says Rosie, tugging my sleeve. "Let's get our skates and go blading. It's a perfect day now."

"No, wait—" I spot something bright red inside the lot. It's almost hidden by a sheet of old yellow newspaper.

"What's that? Hey, look!" I yell to the guys. They turn around and head back.

"What's what?" Lorenzo says.

I point. "That red thing over there."

"Ah, it's nothin'," Mike says. "Come on, you guys."

"It's not *nothing*," I say. "It's *something*—something red. And it wasn't there yesterday. I bet it's something neat." I squint to get a better look.

"I bet it's something grungy," Mike says back.

"And disgusting," says Shrimp.

"C'mon, Lorenzo, give me a leg up," I tell my brother. "Come *on*."

Lorenzo shoots me a really disgusted look. I poke him in the arm. He holds both hands out to make a step and give me a leg up.

"Luz, what are you *doing?*" Rosie asks.

"I'm going to find out what that red thing is," I tell her.

"You're really gonna get it, Luz," Rosie says. "You're *really* gonna get in trouble!"

"There's no stopping her now," Lorenzo says with a big sigh. "I just hope Mami doesn't find out, or the two of us will be grounded forever."

I dig the toes of my high-tops into the chain fence and climb it like a ladder. It's much higher than I thought.

I finally make it up to the top, and over. My hands hurt from holding onto the fence, so I climb down the other side really fast.

Then I jump down and run right over to the old piece of newspaper, past old cans and bedsprings and stuff. I kick the paper away. And there, right in the middle of all that junk and dirt, is a bright red tulip. It's almost as big as a teacup. It's wide open in the sun. One perfect drop of rain shines inside like a diamond. Just like in a movie! I think to myself.

Maybe there was a garden here once, I think as I kneel beside the tulip.

"See, you guys?" I call to the kids. They're all lined up right outside the fence, staring at me like I'm totally nuts. "See? We *can* make a garden grow here. I bet somebody planted this flower years and years ago. And here it is blooming all over again without anybody even helping."

We get so busy arguing about whether there was a

- -

garden here that we don't notice the patrol car glid-ing to a stop at the corner.

Then two police officers get out and slam the doors. In two seconds, they're on the other side of the fence, glaring at me.

"Hey! What do you think you're doing in there?" the first officer hollers at me. She has all this bushy red hair that she keeps pushing up under her cap and she looks about six feet tall. The second officer doesn't say anything.

"Hey, kid! Get over here," the first officer orders.

For a second, I'm too scared to move. Then, before she can say it again, I get up. I walk back to the fence as fast as I can. As I get closer I can see that her name tag says OFFICER CARTER. Her partner's tag says OFFICER RAMIREZ.

By the time I get to the fence, my knees are shak-ing so much I feel like I might fall down. And there I am, trapped.

Uh-oh, I say to myself. What now?

KEEP OUT!

"CAN'T YOU READ?" Officer Carter asks me. Her voice is hard as nails. She points at the rusty sign on the fence. It says KEEP OUT. NO TRESPASSING BY ORDER OF LAW.

My knees and hands are shaking even harder. I know my voice will shake, too, if I try to say anything. But I don't even try. My mouth feels dry as an old washrag.

"You know how dangerous it is in there?" Officer Carter shouts at me. "You could cut yourself and get seriously hurt." She taps her fingers on her nightstick. "If we ever catch you in here again, we'll have to speak to your parents. And you know they won't like that."

I know she's right. It makes me feel even worse.

"Come on, now, climb out of there," Officer Ramirez says. "I'll give you a hand."

He doesn't yell like Carter, but he looks mad anyway. She's still glaring at me, still tapping her fingers.

Officer Ramirez climbs up the other side of the fence so he can help me over. It's a much harder climb this time because my legs are so shaky. I can feel all the kids watching me. Once I get near the top Officer Ramirez grabs my hands to steady me and pulls me over.

Finally, I'm back on the sidewalk. Officer Ramirez bends down and brushes the dirt off the knees of my jeans. "No kidding," he says. "You could get really hurt fooling around in there. What were you doing, anyway?"

I have to clear my throat a few times before any words can come out.

"I saw something red. Something growing. It's—it's a tulip," I say, pointing at it. And I try to explain.

"You see, I've been thinking. This old lot—well, it doesn't have to stay all crummy like this. I was thinking maybe . . . maybe we could turn it into a garden."

Officer Carter gives a little snort. She pushes at her red bushy hair.

"A garden? You gotta be joking. How can you make a garden out of this rattrap?"

I start to shake again. But this time, it's because I'm getting mad.

"*We* didn't throw all that junk in there," I tell her. "It's not *our* fault it's such a mess. But that doesn't mean we couldn't fix it up."

Officer Carter shrugs, turns her back on me, and marches back to the patrol car. She gets in and slams the door.

Officer Ramirez scratches his head, then starts giving a long list of reasons why it can't happen— reasons I've already heard from Lorenzo, Mami, and Rosie. Reasons that all start with "But." And the last and biggest one is always, "But you're only kids."

"I know we're 'only' kids," I tell him. "But that doesn't mean we can't do it. That doesn't mean we're dumb or stupid or bad or something."

Ramirez rubs his scraggly eyebrows and looks me over like he's trying to figure out how serious I am. I want to convince him, so I keep talking.

"We need a place to hang out. Someplace that's not all streets and sidewalks. Someplace pretty."

"Yeah, I think I know what you mean," Ramirez says slowly. "I grew up around here, too. I always hated all the garbage and graffiti. And we always wanted a place to hang out."

He stops for a minute to think. "Listen, there's a group of people called the Green Giants. Maybe you should talk to them."

"What for?" I ask him.

"Well, they help people who want to make gardens," Ramirez explains. "If they decide to sponsor you—now, I'm saying *if* they do—they give you seeds, soil, shovels . . . the kinds of stuff you need."

"Really?"

"Wait—not so fast. Don't get your hopes up," Ramirez warns. He tips his cap back and stares down at me.

"I never heard of them working with kids before. Besides, the city may not even let you use this lot for a garden. You have to find out first."

"How?"

"Call up the Green Giants."

"How do I get the number?" I ask.

"I think I have it," Ramirez mumbles. He pulls out a beat-up notebook. He licks his finger and flips through it for what feels like about an hour and a half. Finally, he finds the Green Giants' number. Then he finds a pen and starts searching all his pockets for a piece of paper. "They should be open Monday."

Officer Carter knocks on the patrol car window and yells, "Come on!"

"Just a second," Ramirez calls back. Carter starts the motor. "Anybody got paper?" he asks.

Nobody does.

"I don't need paper," I tell him. I borrow his pen and write the phone number on my hand. I check twice to make sure I got it right.

I turn to look at Rosie. But she's staring at the ground. Mike, DeVonn, and Shrimp all look away from me. Lorenzo looks right at me but shakes his head.

"We gotta go, Luz," Mike says, heading down the street.

DeVonn follows. "Yeah, we gotta get ready for Little League."

Shrimp trails after them without saying a word. Lorenzo shakes his head again and crosses the street. Then he stands on the corner for a second, waiting for me. Watching. When I don't come, he gives a little wave and walks away.

Rosie goes toward the corner, then turns, like maybe she wants me to catch up with her.

Carter guns the motor and beeps the horn. "Come on, Ramirez. We gotta push off."

"Okay, okay," Ramirez says, getting back in the car and rolling down the window a few inches.

"Looks like it's up to you, kid," Officer Ramirez says.

I look at the telephone number on my hand.

"Good luck," Ramirez says. And the patrol car drives away.

I just stand there, thinking.

I feel a tug on my shirt. It's Rosie, trying to pull me away.

"Come on, Luz, let's go," Rosie says. "Let's go skating."

I stare at the red flower, still glowing in the sun.

"Why don't you just forget it, Luz?" Rosie says.

"I don't want to forget it, Rosie," I tell her. "I want a garden."

Then I say softly, "I wish you'd help me. It'll be worth all the work. You'll see."

"Well, it won't be worth it to me when I have to move a hundred and seventy-five thousand miles away," Rosie says. "By the time that garden's finished— if it ever gets *started*—I won't even be around to enjoy it. And you know it."

Rosie turns her back on me and stomps off.

I watch Rosie disappear around the corner. Now I'm all by myself, standing by the fence with a big gray all-alone feeling.

6 THE GREEN GIANTS

AS SOON AS school gets out Monday, I race home. I sit by the phone trying to get the guts to call the Green Giants. Will they even *talk* to a kid? I wonder.

I pick up the phone. Then I put it down again. I really hate calling people I don't know, especially grown-ups. Unless they're really nice I end up feeling about six inches tall.

The phone number on my hand is almost gone, but I know it by heart. I take a deep breath and punch in the number.

Then I hang up quick before anyone answers. I'm so scared I don't know what to say. I make myself try again. This time I decide exactly what I'm going to say. I dial again and hold on till a woman answers, "Green Giants, Ms. Kline speaking." She sounds cheerful but busy.

I take a deep breath. "I—I want to turn an empty lot into a garden," I say.

"Wonderful," Ms. Kline says. "I can tell you exactly what you need to do. Our first step is to find out if the lot can be used for a garden. The Green Giants will check that for you with the city if you know the exact address."

I love that she said "*Our* first step."

"I do know the exact address," I tell her. I'm glad I double-checked on my way home. "It's on the northeast corner of Sycamore Street and Emerson Avenue—right next to Number 348."

"You're sure?" Ms. Kline asks briskly.

"Sure I'm sure," I say. I can hear her computer keys clicking as she types the address.

"As soon as I know if that lot's available, I'll send you an application form."

"How will you know?" I ask.

"We have to check the records downtown," Ms. Kline says. "It takes a while."

"How long?"

"As long as it takes, dear." Ms. Kline starts to sound a little impatient. "We are very busy this time of year."

"Well, then what happens?" I don't want her to think I'm too pushy, but I can't wait.

"If the lot's available, the Green Giants will help you rent it from the city for only one dollar a year."

"One dollar a year!" I can hardly believe my ears.

"You supply the people, and we supply everything else: from trash collection to supplies. The Green Giants will give you soil, seeds, shovels, work gloves, even trees and bushes to plant."

In my mind, I'm already digging up the soil and planting rosebushes. But she keeps talking.

"But the Green Giants will have to approve your

community group before we agree to sponsor you."

"Oh." I swallow hard. What happens when she finds out I'm not a group? That I'm just one kid?

Then I start thinking. Fast. If I can get the lot, maybe I can get a community group, too. At least I can try.

"Will you send the application today? Right away?" I ask.

"As soon as we know if you can use that lot," Ms. Kline says. "Just a minute, please." I hear her cover the phone with her hand and whisper something. Then she's back.

"Hello?" Ms. Kline clears her throat and asks, "Uh . . . can you please tell me exactly how old you are, dear?"

"Eight and eleven-twelfths," I say.

There's a long pause.

"I see. Well, the Green Giants require at least two responsible adults to sign each application. And we require a group of at least four to six people."

"Oh, no problem," I tell her. I try to put a smile in my voice. "My group is called the . . . the Dream Garden Group! I'll have lots and lots of help."

"Well, I hope so," she says. "It's a big job and you'll need it. But first things first—I have to check on that lot. Then I'll be in touch by mail."

She quickly takes my full name, phone number, and address.

Then she says good-bye and hangs up.

FIRST THINGS FIRST

FOR THE REST of the week I race home after school, hoping to find a letter.

Finally, on Friday, there it is: a fat, creamy-white envelope with a drawing of a bright green giant in the corner. It's sitting on our kitchen table with my name, Ms. Luz Mendes, typed right on the front.

Mami gives me a look that says, "I still don't like this." I try smiling at her, but she won't smile back. So I take the envelope into my room and close the door.

I sit cross-legged on my bed, wishing Rosie were with me. But I didn't see Rosie much this week. And every time I did, she was skating with some girl who lives down the next block.

I look at the envelope with the green giant. But I'm afraid to open it. What if I can't use the lot? What if somebody's already planning to build a house or a store there? My garden will die before it even gets planted.

Finally, I just have to find out. I tear open the envelope and read the letter as fast as I can. There are lots of long words.

> According to official records, the corner lot adjoin-
> ing 348 Emerson Avenue belongs to the City of—

Blah-blah-blah. I keep reading.

> The city government is authorized to lease this
> property for the sum of $1 per year to—

Yay! It's available!

> —a community group approved by the Green
> Giants.

What community group? So far, it's a group of one:
me! There's more.

> In order to apply for sponsorship by the Green
> Giants, fill out the enclosed application in its
> entirety. PLEASE PRINT.

I use my very best printing to fill in all the blanks I
can. Next to COMMUNITY GROUP, I write THE DREAM
GARDEN GROUP. I use my best script to sign my name
on one of the blanks marked MEMBERS.

But there are lots of empty blanks. I still have to
figure out how to get more signatures. But first things
first. I need "two responsible adults."

I'm pretty sure Papi will sign. But I don't know
about Mami. I think for a while, then make up a
plan. I put it right into action.

I go into the kitchen, where Mami is cooking dinner.
Without saying a word about the application, I do every
single thing I'm supposed to. Without even being asked.

I wash my hands, set the table, and help Mami
carry bowls from the stove to the table. I say please
and thank you, and chew every bite of dinner with

my mouth closed. I help clear the table and do the dishes. I spread out my books and start my homework on the kitchen table.

Mami finishes putting away the last pots and pans. Then she sits down at the table across from me. She stirs her hot cup of *café con leche* and takes a sip. I take out the Green Giants application.

"See what I got in the mail today, Mami?" I hold it out, but she won't take it. So I hold it up for her to see. Papi sits down next to me at the table and listens. Lorenzo's door is open, and I can see him at his desk. Listening to every word.

"I got this letter today," I tell Mami. "It's from a group called the Green Giants. They'll help us rent that empty lot on the corner from the city for one dollar a year. Just one dollar, Mami! And they'll give us everything we need to make a garden. A real garden."

Now Mami takes the letter and starts reading. She looks surprised. Her big dark eyes glance up at me, then go on reading.

"I filled out the whole application myself, Mami, see?"

Mami takes it and unfolds it carefully. She smooths it flat with her hand, then takes another sip of her coffee.

"But I need two grown-ups to sign. Will you, Mami? Please?"

Mami stirs her coffee a few times, then looks me

straight in the eye and says, "No." Very quietly, but like she really means it.

"I told you, Luz. That lot is dangerous. I don't want you in there."

I lean across the table and try really hard to convince her.

"I know you don't want me to get hurt, Mami. And I'll be careful. Really careful. I even thought up ways to keep from getting hurt. I can wear my long blue jeans, with boots. And thick gloves, so I won't cut my hands."

Papi clears his throat. "That sounds like a good plan, Luzita. Just be sure to stick to it." He looks at Mami. "I'm going to sign, Lucilla. I think Luz can do this."

Papi picks up the pen. I point to the line where grown-ups sign. My finger shakes just a tiny bit.

Papi can hold a screwdriver or a wrench or a hammer and make them do anything he wants. But he holds a pen in his thick fingers like a first-grader just learning to write.

Papi presses his lips between his teeth and signs Wilfredo Lorenzo Mendes. Then he passes the paper and pen back to me.

I hold it out again to Mami. The back of my throat starts aching, and my eyes start to prickle. I try to fight back the tears, but there are too many of them. They crowd into my eyes and throat, then spill down my cheeks.

"Mami, I wish you could understand how much I want a garden. A real garden—just like your own papi's garden. Remember, Mami? You took me and Lorenzo to Lito's all the time when I was little. When we still lived in Puerto Rico."

Mami doesn't say anything, but I can tell she's listening. So I keep talking, trying to explain.

"Remember the flowers, taller than my head? And the cool green grass? All the trees? And '¡*Coquí! ¡Coquí!*' singing everywhere! It was like a magic place. I still dream of it at night."

From the look in her eyes, I can tell she remembers, too.

"The Green Giants will give us everything we need. Gloves to protect our hands. Garbage bags. Seeds. Soil. And the first thing we'll do is get rid of all the junk. They'll even send a special garbage truck to take it away. We have a chance to make a garden like Lito's, Mami. Our own garden. Right down our street."

The kitchen gets very quiet. The broken faucet that Papi already fixed drips again. Mami sighs and looks in her empty cup. She looks at Papi with her big black eyes. Then she looks at me.

"*Sí*," she says softly. Her voice has a worried little edge to it. But she picks up the pen and signs Lucilla María Mendes. Her letters are round and fancy; they lean toward Papi's as if they want to be nice and close.

Then she folds the application carefully and hands it to me.

"Thank you, Mami!" I snuffle my tears away and give her a big, hard hug. I hug Papi, too. "And I promise I'll be careful."

Lorenzo walks slowly out of his room. I can tell he heard every word.

I look at him, but he shakes his head. "This is your thing, not mine, Luz. If I sign, it's like making a promise I'm not sure I can keep. Sorry."

I can tell he means it. "Well, I'm going to try to change your mind," I say. "But I can't waste time trying to convince you right now. I've got to send this application back right away so I don't lose that lot."

But before I seal the envelope, I write a note to Ms. Kline on one of those yellow sticky things.

> I only have three people <u>SO FAR</u>.
> But I'll get more!!!!!!!
>> Sincerely,
>> Luz Mendes

Lorenzo watches me lick the stamp and address the envelope. "Come on," he says, "I'll walk you to the mailbox."

We end up running all the way.

8 NINE NOES AND ONLY ONE YES

THAT WEEKEND, I spend almost every minute asking everybody I know to join my group and help with the garden. I even ask a few people I don't know that well, like Ali and Nahim who run the bodega next to the lot.

I give people about a hundred reasons why it's a great idea. But everybody's either too busy, or they don't seem to care.

Of course, I wouldn't even dream of asking Rosie. I know she won't help. She hardly even talks to me. All weekend, whenever I meet her on our stoop or running up the stairs in our building, she just ducks her head and pretends she doesn't see me. By the time I can think of something nice to say, she's gone.

I ask Mike, DeVonn, and Shrimp. But they all beg off because of Little League. "We're too busy," Mike says.

"We'll have games and practice all the time once the season starts," Shrimp tells me.

"Yeah, give us a break, Luz," says DeVonn. "It's almost opening day!"

Melinda Park says she thinks it's a great idea, but

she hardly has any time. She goes to Korean school three afternoons a week and takes gymnastics and violin lessons the other two. "I'll try to stop by once in a while, Luz," she tells me. "But I don't think I can help very much."

Early Sunday morning, on my way to church, I see Mrs. Hodges watering the pink geraniums in her first-floor window boxes. She seems to like flowers a lot, so I run up and ask her.

"Sorry, darling," she says in her fancy voice. "But I think these window boxes are quite enough garden for me." Her rings glitter on her hands as she waves good-bye and disappears inside.

Ali and Nahim say they work too hard in the store to work on a garden. "It is a great idea, though," Nahim smiles. "Good luck, Luz."

Then DeVonn Chapman's mom comes into the bodega. I start telling her all about my garden idea. She says she already knows about it from DeVonn. She even looks kind of excited.

"I just love gardens, Luz. We always had one in South Carolina, where I grew up. I'd love to stop by and give you a hand. You just let me know when, honey." She pays for her milk and juice, then stops again on her way out the door. "Just keep in mind that I work a long day before I have to rush home to cook dinner. So I'm not promising I'll always be available—you hear, Luz?" Yeah. I hear. But at least it's not another no!

I go over to Number 45 and try to talk Pony into helping. He listens while he sweeps the sidewalk in front of the building.

"Want to join my Dream Garden Group, Pony? We're gonna make a garden in that old lot on the corner. It'll be awesome. Once it's finished, you can sit there and rest your feet after standing at the door all day," I tell him.

But before he has a chance to answer, one of the fancy blue-haired ladies who live in his building marches up to the door. She clears her throat and waits for Pony to open it.

"*Un momento, Luzita*," Pony says softly to me in Spanish. Then, "Good morning, Mrs. Davidson!" he says out loud to the lady. He runs over to hold the door open while she walks inside like some sort of queen or president.

"Your garden's a great idea, Luz," Pony tells me as soon as she's gone. "But I can't promise anything. I never know from one week to the next whether I'm working night shift or day shift. Sorry."

And that's the way it goes with everybody. So here it is, late Sunday afternoon, and all I have are nine noes, one yes, and a lot of maybes. That'll go over like a lead balloon when Ms. Kline calls to find out how many people are in my group.

I sit on my stoop, trying to decide what to do next. And who do you think comes walking down the street?

Rosie and her mom. Rosie and I haven't really talked or hung out together since the day we had that big fight about the garden.

Now she at least waves at me. She even says hi if we bump into each other. But she doesn't ask me to play anymore. She never comes and rings my bell.

And I've been afraid to ring hers. What if she slams the door in my face? What if she sees me through the peephole and won't even answer? It feels like forever since we went up on my roof to giggle and sing and watch the sky.

Rosie and her mom are coming closer now. My stomach is clutching, because I'm afraid Rosie won't even say hi. I almost get up and run inside. Then I see her coming up to me with that nice little smile she gets on her face.

"Hi, Luz," her mom says, and goes inside.

"I'll be home soon, Mom," Rosie calls out.

Then she sits down beside me on our favorite step. "Hi, Luz, how are you?"

"Great," I say. It's true I was feeling kind of down about the garden. But now that Rosie's here, I'm starting to cheer up. And I know that the garden is

----

the last thing in the world I should talk about with Rosie.

"Whatcha doing?"

"Not much. Just sitting here."

"Listen, Luz. My mom's taking me out for brunch and the movies some Saturday before we move—as a special treat. She said you could come. Want to?"

"Sure! I'd love to."

"Great," says Rosie. It makes me happy to see her blue eyes twinkling behind her glasses. And before we know it, we're jabbering away just like we always do. I can tell Rosie feels as happy as I do about being friends again.

"Hey, Rosie," I say. "I have a great idea."

She looks at me and then we both burst out laughing.

"Let's go up—" I start.

"—and watch the sunset," she finishes.

We're on our feet before the words are out of our mouths. We race up all five flights of stairs, all the way up to the roof. We stay there till we can make a wish on the first star.

9 TRUCE

ROSIE AND I start hanging out again every day after school. Some days we skate. Others, we go up on the roof or down in front of our house to play double Dutch or soccer. Sometimes we get DeVonn and Shrimp to play, too.

By now, it's really spring. The sun is hotter, the air is warmer, and most days we don't need sweaters. Bright yellow-green leaves poke out on the scrawny trees on our street. A few skinny weeds grow in the cracks of the sidewalk. The geraniums in Mrs. Hodges's window boxes get bigger and brighter.

But there's still no real garden in our neighborhood. If you don't look in the right places, you'll miss spring completely.

Then, one day—a few weeks after I mailed my application to the Green Giants—Rosie and I are running upstairs to my apartment. We're laughing our heads off at some silly knock-knock jokes we're making up. Then we hear the phone in my kitchen ringing and ringing.

I put my key in the lock as fast as I can. We burst in the door, all out of breath and giggling. I pick up the phone in the middle of a ring. And I almost collapse on the kitchen floor.

"It's Ms. Kline!" I whisper to Rosie. "The Green Giants lady."

Luckily, Ms. Kline does most of the talking while I catch my breath. I see Rosie stop laughing. She just stands there and watches me with a strange look on her face.

"Can you meet me Saturday morning at nine to start cleaning up the lot?" says Ms. Kline.

"Saturday morning? Sure!" I say.

"I'm still worried about the size of your group," Ms. Kline says, "but the weather's so nice, I'd like to get you started."

"Oh, don't worry, Ms. Kline. I have one more yes!" I look at Rosie with a big question on my face, but Rosie shakes her head no! and turns away. "Mrs. Chapman from over on Dooley wants to join the group, Ms. Kline. She says she'll sign the application."

"That's better, Luz, but we need more than maybes. Well, I'll be there Saturday to help you get started. Lots of times more people get interested once we get the ball rolling. See you at nine sharp?"

"Nine sharp. And I'll keep trying, Ms. Kline. I promise!"

I hang up, let out a yell, and give Rosie a bear hug. Then I grab her hands and dance her all around the kitchen.

"We start cleaning up the lot Saturday morning!" I tell Rosie. "Then Ms. Kline will give me and Papi the key. That means we can go in and work on the garden whenever we want! You'll help, won't you, Rosie? Please? It won't be the same without you."

Rosie stops whirling and pushes me away. I keep dancing and spinning, hugging Rosie, the chairs, the refrigerator—whatever I can get my hands on.

"We did it!" I yell. I'm so happy, I'm nearly flying.

But Rosie isn't happy. Not one bit. Even the little freckles on her little nose look mad and hurt. I finally stand still and watch her.

"Saturday morning? *This* Saturday?" Rosie says. She starts walking toward the door. Halfway across the kitchen, she turns and looks at me.

"You forgot, didn't you?" Rosie's voice is so sharp it hurts. "Saturday's when we're going out for brunch and the movies with my mom. Remember? We planned the whole thing already, Luz."

Rosie's right. I did forget. It's written all over my face.

"See? You care more about your dumb, stupid old garden than you do about me." Rosie's big blue eyes get all shiny from tears.

"No, I don't, Rosie. I was just so excited that—"

"Well, I'll just find somebody else to go to the movies and have fun with. Somebody who doesn't care a thing about gardens."

Tears start to spill down Rosie's cheeks. She runs out of my kitchen and stomps down the stairs.

She doesn't even look back, so she never sees the tears running down my cheeks, too.

CLEANUP DAY

SATURDAY'S BRIGHT AND sunny. My eyes pop
open way before my alarm rings. And I know right away
why I'm so happy: It's the very first day of my garden.
It's not a dream anymore!

I run to my window and do a little dance in
a warm patch of sunshine. Then I jump into my clothes,
grab one of Mami's sweet rolls, and run down to the
corner to meet Ms. Kline. While I'm waiting, I look for
the red tulip. There it is, blooming away in the middle
of all the old newspapers and all the junk.

I pace up and down on the sidewalk outside the
fence. I'm the first one there. In fact, I'm the only one
there. And I'm still not sure who will show up.

I can't help wishing Rosie would come. I feel awful
about our fight. But I'm not sure how to say sorry.
That's because I'm still mad at her, too. I know it's hard
for her to think about moving away. But it's hard for me
to lose her. Especially when she's still living right downstairs.

But I can't think about Rosie right now. Because I see
a lady who might be Ms. Kline. She's parking an old,
beat-up car near the corner. She gets out and starts to
unload stuff—rakes and brooms, big plastic bags, lots of
work gloves.

She's sort of round and plump. Wisps of gray hair poke out from under her big straw hat. She's wearing an old sweatshirt and jeans. Her sneakers are full of mud.

"Hi!" I say, and wave both hands.

"Luz? Luz Mendes?" she calls out to me.

"Hi, Ms. Kline. Want some help?"

"You bet." She's having trouble balancing all her stuff. The rakes fall with a clatter when she tries to pick up the brooms.

I run and grab the rakes with my left hand, then hold out my right hand to shake. I try to look as grown-up as I can.

"Glad to meet you, Luz." Ms. Kline smiles. Then she looks around to see who else is with me.

Nobody. Yet.

She stares down at me through her thick glasses, then looks up and down the block again. As if maybe she somehow missed seeing all the people in that big Dream Garden Group I'm supposed to have. She clears her throat.

"Uh—where is everybody?" Ms. Kline asks.

"They're not here. Yet. But don't worry," I tell her, trying not to look one bit worried myself. "The Dream Garden Group is on its way. And I'm very, *very* energetic. You'll see!" I pick up another rake to show how much I mean it.

Ms. Kline gives me one of those tiny grown-up smiles that's just pretend-friendly. It makes me feel nervous instead of good.

But then Papi turns the corner, and I start to feel better. I feel even better when Mrs. Chapman shows up right behind him.

The grown-ups shake hands and introduce themselves. Then Ms. Kline gives us all thick work gloves and puts on a pair herself. She takes a key out of her jeans' pocket and sticks it in the rusty padlock. Here's the big moment I've been waiting for! The gate screeches as we push it back. And we're inside!

The four of us get right to work. We start picking up cans and bottles, raking trash out of corners, and shoveling junk into bags.

But it's not like in the movies when you start a hard job and *presto!*—two seconds later it's all done.

No way. After what feels like a million hours, I'm still picking up cans and bottles. Papi is still raking trash out of corners. And Ms. Kline and Mrs. Chapman are still shoveling junk into bags.

Lots of people walk past. Most of them don't even notice what we're doing. And nobody offers to help.

Then, all of the sudden, I see Rosie and her mom turn the corner. My heart rises straight up in my chest.

Yay! I want to shout. You're coming after all!

I wipe my sweaty face on my sleeves. I get ready to run over and open the gate extra wide to let her in. But Rosie doesn't even look at me.

My heart falls down, hard, when she walks right past without even turning her head. She's wearing her favorite denim shirt and a new belt I've never seen.

Get real, I tell myself. Rosie's not coming to help.

She's on her way to pick up that girl from down the block. Then they're going out to brunch and the movies.

I turn around fast so Rosie won't see me watching her. I start picking up cans and bottles and shoving them into my garbage bag. It gives me something to do besides worry about Rosie.

Then—total surprise! My brother, Lorenzo, shows up.

"*¡Hola, Luzita!* Need a hand?"

"I need about a hundred." I grin.

"Well, will you settle for two?" Lorenzo grins back, then puts on gloves and starts picking up stuff. With two of us working side by side, we seem to work more than twice as fast.

"You know, Luz, you got me thinking about Lito and his garden. When you were talking to Mami about *your* dream garden." Lorenzo speaks quietly, but I can hear every word. "I remember how cool it was when we played there. How bright the flowers were. How it almost felt like a magic place."

Lorenzo stops working for a second, and so do I. "You're right, Luz. We do need a garden around here. I'm glad we're doing this."

We go back to work without saying anything else. But the word "we" sings in my ears.

A little later, DeVonn stops by to say hi to his mom. He's wearing his new Little League uniform: a bright yellow Tornados shirt with number 15 on the back, gray pants, yellow socks.

DeVonn watches us pick up more cans and bottles.

Then he parks his catcher's mitt and bat inside the fence and helps out. He tries so hard not to get his uniform dirty that he doesn't get a whole lot done. But it's still fun having him there. He jokes around and makes the time go faster.

"Whoops," he says when the church bells chime eleven. "I gotta go warm up for my game. Don't work too hard, you guys."

"Thanks, DeVonn," I call out. "Can you come back later?"

"I don't think so," he says. "I gotta meet Mike."

I go right back to work—bend and pick, shove and push, bend and pick. Soon I can hardly remember ever doing anything else.

Around noon, Papi brings us cold juice and hot Cuban sandwiches from the bodega next door. We all eat together on the sidewalk, too tired to talk much.

I count eighteen huge garbage bags piled up at the curb. I've got blisters on my hands, sunburn on my nose, and aches in strange muscles I never knew I had. But the lot still looks like a junk heap.

When it's time to get started again, my legs are so stiff I can hardly get up. But I don't want to act chicken, so I'm the first one back to work. The others follow me slowly.

Finally, around three o'clock, Ms. Kline puts down her rake.

"I've had it," she says.

"Me, too," Mrs. Chapman groans, rubbing her shoulders.

I've never been so tired in my whole life. But I'm

afraid to say one word of complaint. Otherwise, Ms. Kline will think I can't do this. And I'm trying so hard to convince her!

Now I count twenty-eight bags stuffed with garbage. Most of the small junk is gone. Papi and Ms. Kline drag the bedsprings and other big stuff out to the curb where the garbage truck can pick it up Monday morning.

I look around the lot. You can actually see the ground! And there's the red tulip, standing straight up in the middle. No old newspapers hide it now. It waves in the wind like a brave red flag that says, "You can do it! You can!" But we still have a long way to go.

"Well, Luz, you certainly are energetic." Ms. Kline stretches her back. "But you've still got to get more people to help." She frowns at me. But at least it's not one of those pretend smiles. She thinks for a minute, then digs in her pocket for the key. She dangles it in the air.

"I'm going to give this key to you and your papi, Luz. I'll be back next Saturday to see how much progress your group has made."

She sighs. "If you can't get this place cleaned up by then, the Green Giants just can't sponsor you. I'll have to take back the key and lock up this place for good."

I try to smile. "Don't worry, Ms. Kline, we'll do it. I'll get lots of people to help. You'll see."

I only hope I'm right.

WORRY WEEK

THAT NIGHT I realize I only have six days to get the lot cleaned up *and* come up with the rest of the Dream Garden Group. Otherwise, Ms. Kline will take back the key and lock up the lot for good. I know I'll have to spend every spare minute either working on the garden or trying to convince other people to help me.

On Sunday, Mami forbids me to go anywhere near the garden. Instead, I have to get all dressed up and go to Mass. Then I have to help Mami for the rest of the day while about a dozen of my most boring relatives come for dinner.

On Monday, I rush home after school, change into my grungy clothes, grab my gloves and key, and go to work. Whenever somebody I know walks by, I invite them to come in, look around, maybe even give me a hand. But Mrs. Chapman and Papi are my only helpers. We fill two more bags with cans and bottles before it's time for supper and homework.

On Tuesday, Lorenzo, DeVonn, and Shrimp help for about an hour before it starts pouring. We get most of the old newspapers picked up and stuffed into bags.

On Wednesday, Lorenzo drags Mike over. "How's

Luz's nightmare?" Mike teases. But Lorenzo convinces him to come in and help pick up the last of the bottles. For a grand total of twenty minutes. After he leaves, Lorenzo and I start raking chunks of glass out of the weeds near the fence. Papi stops by to help.

On Thursday, I see Kenya and Shuwanza, two first-grade girls from my school, playing hopscotch across the street. They're real curious when they see me open the gate. "Want to come in?" I yell. "We're making this into a garden. You can help if you want."

They come in and help me rake leaves. But after about half an hour they get tired and start giggling and go back to their game.

"Maybe we'll come back tomorrow," says Kenya. Maybe.

On Friday, Lorenzo and DeVonn help after school till suppertime. Melinda Park stops in to help after her violin lesson. We rake the last of the trash out of the corners. DeVonn says, "This place is starting to look much better, you guys." We all agree.

My papi was the only one I could count on to show up every single day—even if it was only for a few minutes after work. But as the week went by, I noticed more and more people stopping to watch instead of just walking past.

Some even offered free advice. "Don't forget, you'll need some nice, rich topsoil before you can grow anything in there," Mrs. Hodges told me.

"That lot is looking much nicer, Luz," Mrs. Pazzalini calls out as we're getting ready to leave late Friday afternoon.

"Want to help, Mrs. P.?" I call back.

"I can't now, dear. I'm running to the bookstore. Maybe some other time." But I can't tell if "some other time" will ever come.

I make sure to tell everybody who stops to show up tomorrow morning when the lady from the Green Giants will be here again. But—you guessed it—I still get mostly maybes.

One thing I do know: Rosie still won't help. Not even a little. She skates by a lot—sometimes by herself, sometimes with the girl down the block. She sees me, all right. But she doesn't come in. She hardly even says hi.

On Saturday morning, Lorenzo and I race over to the lot extra early to make sure things look really great for Ms. Kline.

Lorenzo beats me to the corner. Then he stops short, and I bump right into him.

"Oh, no!" he groans. "Look at that."

I can't believe what I see. During the night—after we locked up to go home for supper yesterday— somebody dropped a whole, huge load of garbage over the fence. Soda cans, rotten salad, yucky old coffee grounds, eggshells. And stacks and stacks of newspapers, which the wind blew all around during

the night. Ripped pages are stuck in the fence and flying like dirty flags near the wall.

"Oh, no! What a mess." I sigh. Lorenzo just shakes his head. "C'mon," I say. "We better get busy."

We unlock the padlock and push open the gate. We grab two garbage bags and rake stuff in as fast we can. We've got to get this cleaned up before Ms. Kline comes!

Just then, Mike, DeVonn, and Shrimp pass by on their way to baseball practice. "Hey, what happened?" Shrimp calls. "I thought we finished cleaning up this place already."

"We did," I call back. "But now we have to do it again. And we have to do it fast, before Ms. Kline shows up. If she sees this mess, she'll take back the key, lock up the lot, and good-bye garden."

"Want some help?" DeVonn asks. Without waiting for an answer, he and Shrimp come in and get busy.

Mike yells to them, "Hey, what do you guys think you're doing? We've got practice in half an hour."

"So we'll help for half an hour," DeVonn says. "Keep your baseball shirt on, Mike. We'll get there in time to win the pennant." Mike turns his hat backward on his head. He stands there punching his mitt to break it in. Then he comes in, too. We all keep stuffing the new trash into bags as fast as we can.

Mrs. Hodges passes by, walking her little white poodle with the pink hair bows. When she sees what happened, she ties her dog's leash to the fence. "Now you stay right there while Mama helps clean up," she says in fake baby talk. Then she picks up a rake and gets busy.

When Lorenzo sees I have plenty of help, he dashes to the gate. "I'm going for Papi, Luz. We'll be right back." I'm too busy to answer.

Mrs. Chapman and DeVonn's big sister, Keisha, pass by on their way home from the supermarket. Mrs. Chapman takes one look and clicks her tongue. "Look at that mess!" she says.

"Come on, Mom," DeVonn yells. "We need you!"

Mrs. Chapman taps Keisha on the shoulder. They both come in, set down their grocery bags, and get right to work.

Lorenzo and Papi come back with Pony. "We caught him on his way home from the night shift," Lorenzo explains quickly. He hands Pony a garbage bag and all three of them start picking up newspapers.

Soon, about a dozen people are busy stuffing the last of the new garbage into bags, tying them closed, and hauling them out of the lot.

And just in time! We're stacking the last of the bags by the curb when Ms. Kline's old rattletrap car turns the corner.

She gets out and slams the door. She's wearing exactly the same clothes as last week. She pushes that old straw hat back on her head and stands there grinning, hands on hips.

I meet her at the gate. "Good morning, Ms. K.," I say in my happiest voice.

"Good morning, Luz. Well, I must admit I'm pretty impressed. I see your Dream Garden Group isn't just a pipe dream after all."

Ms. Kline sounds like she can hardly believe it. No wonder. I can hardly believe it myself!

"You've got quite a work crew this week. And your garden looks just about ready for planting."

It's true. Almost every scrap of trash is gone. Most of the broken glass is raked out of the dirt. There's a bunch of big green weeds sticking up over by the wall, but that just makes it look more like a garden.

Ms. Kline looks around one more time, then looks me straight in the eye. This time her smile is one hundred percent real.

"Well, if you've got your one dollar rent, Luz, I guess you and your Dream Garden Group will be in business!"

I dig down into my jeans and pull out a carefully folded one-dollar bill. I smooth it out and hand it to Ms. Kline. We shake. Then I break into a yell and do a victory dance up and down the sidewalk.

Mrs. Chapman, DeVonn, and Keisha clap and cheer. "Bravo! *Bravissimo!*" Mrs. Hodges calls out in her fancy voice. Mike lets out an earsplitting whistle. Shrimp yells, "Hurray!"

Everybody crowds around, shaking my hands and clapping me on the back. And suddenly, everybody is full of ideas about what to plant, and where.

The only thing missing is Rosie.

DELIVERY DAY

THE WHOLE NEXT week, I work on a map of our garden. I study the Green Giants catalog that shows all the stuff we can order. There are pages and pages of bright-colored flowers, all kinds of trees, and pictures of the most scrumptious vegetables you ever saw.

I bring the catalog down to our stoop after school and ask people in the Dream Garden Group to help decide what to get. I use chalk to sketch different ideas on the sidewalk. I figure lots of people will stop by and help. And that's just what happens. Before long, we pick out what we want and I call in our order to Ms. Kline.

Then suddenly it's next Saturday. Delivery day. I run to open the gate at nine sharp. But this time, I'm not alone! Lots of people are there to help: Papi and Lorenzo, the Chapmans, the Pazzalinis, Melinda Park, Mrs. Hodges (and her dog), even Mike. Pony stops by on his way home from the night shift. There's a big buzz of talk, and lots of laughing. Everybody says good morning when Ms. Kline comes.

Best of all, Mami shows up! Right now she's standing outside the fence, as if she's not quite sure whether to come in or leave.

I feel like a big deal, standing by the gate when the delivery truck pulls up. It's much bigger than I expected. And it's right on time. A tall, husky man climbs out and checks some papers.

"I'm lookin' for Mrs. Luz Mendes," he calls out. "Is she here?"

Everybody laughs, and the man looks a little confused.

"Anybody know where Mrs. Luz Mendes is?" he says, scratching his head.

I feel myself turn bright red. Then I get up my courage and walk to the front of the crowd. But the man is looking right over my head. He doesn't even notice me. I make myself as tall as I can and tap him on the elbow.

"Hi," I say. "I'm *Ms.* Luz Mendes."

He looks down at me, totally surprised. I guess he never made a delivery to a kid before.

"Well, I guess you better sign here," he says. I use my very best script.

"Okay, Pete—you ready? Let's unload," he calls to his helper.

We all watch the back of the huge truck swing open. Inside, we can see giant bags full of soil and sand. There are piles of lumber, big cans of bright green paint, buckets, boxes of tools and supplies, packets of flower and vegetable seeds, and dozens of teeny tiny little plants called seedlings. There are even real live trees and bushes!

Papi and Mr. Pazzalini help the men unload the truck. Other people help carry everything into the garden. Everyone asks me where to put things. I look at my map and tell them, "Boards and paint over by the wall, please. Sand in the middle. Soil along the fence."

When I look up, I catch a glimpse of Mami. She's still watching me. I can see a little smile start to perk up her mouth. Then it reaches her eyes. It's like someone turned on a happy switch when that light starts shining in her eyes.

Then come the trees—eight of them! Two apple, two cherry, two sycamore, and two maple. Tags show their names and pictures of them. We'll have pink and white in the spring; green all summer; and red and gold in the fall. I get so excited telling the men where to put each tree that I forget to watch Mami watching me.

Then I turn around—and there she is, right beside me. She reaches out and gives me a quick, hard hug. "Ah, Luzita, I am so proud of you! So proud! ¡Qué orgullosa me siento! I wish Lito could see you and your garden!"

I feel at least six feet tall.

The empty truck pulls away with a roar. The delivery guys lean out the windows and wave. "Go, Luz!" they yell. "Lotsa luck!"

Now Papi gets busy measuring and sawing and hammering benches. Mr. Pazzalini, Shrimp, and Pony work on the vegetable garden. Mrs. Chapman and

- -

Ms. Kline help me measure the flower beds with stakes and string. Even Mami helps!

Lorenzo and DeVonn start digging up the hard, packed-down dirt. They mix in soft, dark topsoil to get the ground ready to plant. Mike horses around a little, but finally gives them a hand.

Then, when Papi says we should water our newly planted trees, I almost panic. I realize something I absolutely, totally forgot: water!

I think fast. Then I grab one of the buckets and run next door to the bodega. Ali shows me where his sink is and says we can use the water whenever we want. "Just don't water my customers," he kids me. I practically have to drag the heavy bucket back to the garden. From then on, people take turns helping get water.

We work all day, but the time flies past. And more and more people come to help out. Soon it seems like half the neighborhood is there, helping this garden happen.

Then, one more surprise. Mami and I are carrying another bucket of water when I hear a *beep-beep!* from the street. At first I pay no attention. Then it comes again—*beep-beep!* This time I turn and look.

I see a blue-and-white patrol car sitting at the curb. Officer Carter is at the wheel, looking impatient and arguing with somebody on her two-way radio.

But Officer Ramirez rolls down his window and waves. I run over. He's smiling from ear to ear.

"Well, well, well," he says, reaching out and shaking

my hand. "Looks like you're a girl who really means what she says, huh?"

"I called the Green Giants, just like you said. It wasn't exactly easy—but here we are." I bow and say, "Ta-da! One super-special Dream Garden coming right up!"

Ramirez puts up his hand for a high five. I give him ten.

Then I get an idea.

"Listen, I've been thinking. We'll probably finish planting the garden next Saturday. Then we're having a big party Saturday night to celebrate. Want to come? You were my very first helper, you know."

Ramirez takes off his cap and bows his head, like to a grown-up lady. "*Muchas gracias, señorita.* I'd be delighted."

The two-way radio buzzes and crackles as Officer Carter signs off. For the first time, she turns to take a really good look at my garden. She stares at the hustle-bustle of all the people working. She watches Mrs. Chapman brush a coat of fresh white paint over the graffiti on the back wall.

"That looks nice, kid. Real nice. I bet your parents are pretty proud of you."

Mami is kneeling behind the fence, chucking stones out of the soil. She doesn't say anything, but I can see her smiling.

Now it seems like everybody in the whole world believes in my dream garden.

Everybody except Rosie.

13 RED SIZZLERS AND PINK PROMISES

THE NEXT SATURDAY morning, DeVonn, Keisha, Shrimp, and Mrs. Chapman are already at the garden when I get there with Lorenzo and Papi. We all stand there for a few minutes, bragging to each other about how much we'd done over the past week. The old bottles and cans are completely gone. The vegetable garden is ready for planting. And the sandbox and benches are nearly finished.

Then we get to work. All morning, people show up to help out; everybody from last week, plus a few new faces.

One by one, trees go into the ground. It takes lots of people: some digging, some lifting, some watering. And lots more standing around making suggestions and giving orders.

Keisha and Melinda are down on their knees planting seedlings—teeny tiny tomato and marigold and petunia plants. Mami and Mrs. Pazzalini are putting in a bed of herbs and stuff for cooking: mint, oregano, basil, chives. Shrimp, Mike, and our sax-playing friend, Salvie, are planting pumpkins for Halloween and Thanksgiving.

I kneel by the fence near the gate, planting baby rosebushes. I chose some for Mami called Red Sizzlers—they looked like big red fireworks in the Green Giants catalog.

But the ones I chose for Rosie are the best. They're called Pink Promises, and they're small and pretty like she is. When they grow, they'll climb up and cover the whole fence. In the catalog, they look like a beautiful pink waterfall. I know Rosie will really like them. *If* she ever comes to the garden. If—

And then I realize: Rosie will never see the pink waterfall of blooming roses—not ever. By the time these bushes grow that big, she'll be living halfway across the country. No wonder she hates this garden. No wonder she's so mad at me.

I sit back on my heels and take a break. Papi's pounding the few last nails into his benches. I go over to watch. "They look great, Papi!"

"Think so, Luzita? Well, let's sit down and test them out." He takes my arm, just like a king leading a princess to her throne. We sit down together on the bench.

My toes can't touch the ground, but the bench feels good and solid. I look up into the branches of a skinny little sycamore tree we just planted. A few lacy leaves wave against the bright blue sky. It's almost like being in the country. Almost like Lito's garden.

"Good benches, Papi." I lean over and give him a big hug. And I whisper in his ear, "*Gracias, Papi.*

Thanks for helping. And especially for believing in my garden."

Papi's eyes crinkle at the corners as he smiles at me. "Are you ready to paint them?"

I jump up. "I'm ready!"

Papi shows me how to use a screwdriver to open a large green can of paint by prying up the lid. Then he gives me a flat wooden stick to stir the paint. I swirl the bright green paint round and round in the can. Green Giant green, I think with a little smile. I dip in a brand-new paintbrush. I love the way the creamy paint turns the tip of the brush bright green.

I brush the first stripe of paint on Papi's bench. I dip my brush again—then a shadow turns the shiny wet paint a darker green.

I look up. There's Rosie, peeking through the fence. Her glasses flash in the sunshine. I can't really see her eyes, so I have no idea what she's thinking.

"It looks real nice," Rosie says. She clears her throat as if it's hard to get the words out. "Your garden looks really great, Luz. Uh . . . need any help?"

"Sure," I say. "Come on in, Rosie."

"Sure it's okay?" Rosie asks.

"Sure." I'm trying to be cool, but my heart is beating fast and happy.

Rosie comes into the garden for the very first time. She looks around at all the people and plants. Then she sits down cross-legged beside me under the skinny little tree. "What should I do?" she asks.

- -

"Want to water those bushes I just planted?"

Rosie jumps up. "Yeah, sure. What are they?"

"They're rosebushes," I say, looking up to watch her face. "I picked them out myself. They're called Pink Promises, and they get little pink roses all over them."

"Pink roses? My favorite," Rosie says.

"Yeah, I know," I say. "That's why I chose them."

Rosie looks from the rosebushes to me.

"I wanted something to help me think of you, even when you move away. And I wanted to find a special way of saying sorry for that day I forgot about the movies."

Rosie doesn't say anything. She just looks down and breaks up a little ball of soil with her fingers.

"I am sorry," I say. "I didn't mean to hurt your feelings. And I think I see why you'd hate working on a garden when you're moving."

Rosie sort of smiles. "Well, I'm not moving for three whole months. We can still have lots of fun before then. Where's the bucket?"

We get the bucket and water the roses. Then we spend the rest of the day painting the benches—and ourselves—Green Giants green.

DREAMS COME TRUE

EVERYBODY LIKED MY idea about having a big neighborhood party to celebrate the garden. We worked all day, planting and watering and weeding, then everybody rushed home to clean up.

I rush through my shower really fast so I can get back to the garden before anybody else. I put on my favorite purple shorts and a new T-shirt Mami got me just for the party.

My freshly washed hair is still dripping down my back when I get back to the garden. But I'm glad I'm there alone for a few minutes. I want to sit on my bench under the sycamore tree and think.

Outside the fence, the sidewalk looks hard and dirty. Busy cars beep and screech past. The Number 5 bus groans to a stop at the corner.

I sit in the cool quiet. All around me is a deep, dark-brown smell I seem to remember from a dream . . . or from Lito's garden. Even the taxi horns seem far away. Everywhere I look, I see pointy green shoots. Our skinny little trees seem to be standing up straighter now. As if the Dream Garden feels like home. As if they're saying, "We live here now. This is our garden, too. Come on in and check us out."

Of course, it's still the West Side. There's litter fluttering against the fence. And even though we locked the gate last night, SPIKE 168 sprayed his name in bright red all over the wall Mrs. Chapman had just painted white yesterday. We don't have another can of paint, so SPIKE 168 has to stay for now.

Maybe someday Spike 168 will come into the garden and see how nice it is to stretch out on this bench under the sycamore tree. Maybe.

Soon neighbors start coming, talking and laughing while they set up for the party. Shrimp helps his mom and dad string colored Christmas lights along the top of the fence. Lorenzo sets up his boom box and starts playing tapes. He tunes his guitar for later.

Papi and Ali bring sawhorses and rest old doors on top. Presto! Tables! Other people bring folding chairs. Mrs. Park puts clean sheets on the "tables" and spreads blankets on the ground for people who want to eat picnic-style.

And here comes the food! Mrs. Chapman and Keisha bring big platters of fried chicken. DeVonn's right behind with a giant bowl of homemade potato salad. Mrs. Pazzalini brings her famous lasagna. Someone else brings sweet potato and blueberry pies, hot from the oven. When Mrs. McCormack marches in with a pot of her famous corned beef and cabbage, she can hardly find a place to put it! There's everything from Lebanese bread to spicy Jamaican curried goat.

Then Mrs. Hodges and Ms. Kline show up carrying a huge sheet cake. Mami takes one look and laughs, "*¡Mira!* Luz, look at this!"

I run over to see the cake. It's frosted pale green, decorated with those different-colored icings you squeeze out of tubes. Ms. Kline drew in grass, trees, even a green bench. There are bright flowers and a huge orange pumpkin. In chocolate writing it says

LONG LIVE OUR DREAM GARDEN!

Now comes the music. Salvie brings his sax. Some guys from up on Dooley set up their steel drums. They all tune up and start jamming. No question: This'll be one great party!

The sun sets in a big red glow. By now, the party's in full swing. People are eating and talking and laughing. Some little kids play in the sandbox, building castles and "baking cakes." Other kids just hang out or fool around together, having a great time. Because you don't actually have to *do* anything to enjoy the garden.

Mike and DeVonn finish eating and start up a game of hide-and-seek. "Come on, Luz," Mike yells, "You're It!"

"Not now, Mike," I call back. I don't want to be hiding or seeking when Rosie shows up. I want to meet her at the gate to show her how happy I am she's here.

But where *is* Rosie?

I go to the corner so I can look down our street or up the avenue for Rosie.

Mr. Pazzalini plugs in the colored lights and turns the switch at the bodega. Everybody says "oooh!" and "ah!"

I see a tall man and an even taller woman get out of a taxi. The man is carrying a big, bulky brown package. I know I've seen that bushy red hair somewhere . . . oh! I almost fall down. It's Officer Carter, wearing a flowery summer dress, high heels, and— biggest surprise of all—a smile! She and Officer Ramirez both look strange and different without their uniforms. But I run to meet them at the gate.

Officer Carter shakes my hand and nods to Officer Ramirez. "A gift for your garden," Ramirez says, handing me the package.

I tear off the brown paper and find a green garden hose coiled up inside. It's the longest hose I've ever seen—long enough to stretch as far as the sink in the bodega.

"Oh, cool! This is a perfect present. Just what we need! Thanks! Thanks a million!" I tell them.

Then I take them on a tour and show them everything.

When Mami spots us, she comes over with a big smile. "Come, help yourselves to food." She leads the way and I start to follow.

Then I catch sight of Rosie walking down Sycamore Street carrying a very big wooden . . . something.

I run to meet her. "Hi! Can I help? That whatever-it-is looks heavy!"

"You can help, but you can't look. Yet." Rosie's little mouth is all smiles. Her glasses catch the glow of the colored lights.

I take one end of the big wooden thing. There are two holes at the top of one of the long sides. Metal shower curtain hooks jingle in the holes. It's about three feet long and two feet wide. The back just looks like an old board. What's on the front? I wonder.

Papi meets us at the gate. "¡Hola, Rosita! Welcome!" He takes the big, heavy board without letting me see the front.

"Want to see the little leaves on your rosebushes?" I ask.

"Yes!" Rosie's all excited. "But your surprise comes first." Her eyes dance behind her glasses. "All right, now, Luz. Close your eyes and don't peek till we tell you. Promise?"

"Promise." I cover my eyes with my hands. I want to look. But this time I keep my promise.

I hear DeVonn yelling, "Hey, Mike! Shrimp! Lorenzo! It's time."

I can hear kids and grown-ups crowding around. Salvie's sax and the steel drums keep playing, but I can tell Lorenzo has put down his guitar. He must be watching, too. I hear Mami whisper; Officer Carter whispers back, but I can't hear the words.

There's rattling and clattering and more whisper-ing. Rosie giggles. Something bumps against the fence just about where I climbed it that very first day. Then Rosie takes my shoulders and spins me around once, twice, three times.

"Okay, Luz, count to three and open your eyes."

And exactly on the count of three, Mike's whistle splits the air. I open my eyes. Rosie's big board is now hanging high up on the fence where everybody can see it. In big red letters it says

LUZ'S GARDEN:
A DREAM COME TRUE

It has a fancy silver border, and the background is purple (my favorite). It's decorated with big yellow sunflowers in all four corners.

For almost the first time in my whole life, I can't say a word. Not a single word. My eyes and my throat are too full of happiness.

I grab Rosie and whirl her around and around. And this time, she doesn't stop me.

Dear Reader,

Would you like to turn an empty lot into a garden? Lots of people—including kids—already have. If you're willing to work hard with your neighbors, you probably can, too!

Community gardening programs all over the country help people by giving them information, soil, seeds, fencing, and other supplies. To find out about the one nearest you, write to:

The American Community Gardening
Association
325 Walnut Street
Philadelphia, PA 19106

Here are some of the other steps you will need to take:
- Find an interested grown-up to help you.
- Find out the exact address of the lot.
- Find out who owns the lot from the Department of Records in your city or town.
- Get the owner's permission to use the lot. (It could be an individual person, a group, or your city or town government.)
- Contact the community gardening program nearest you to ask for help.
- Invite your family, friends, and neighbors to work with you.

I hope you will plant your own dream garden. If you do, please write and tell me about it.

Sincerely yours,

Ellen Schecter